MORE SPECIAL OFF
FOR MR MEN AND LITTLE MIS

D0091814

In every Mr Men and Little Miss book like this (
sticker and activity books, you will find a special to
will send you a gift of your choice
Choose either a <u>Mr Men</u> <u>or</u> <u>Little Miss</u> poster, **or** a Mr Men or Little Miss
double sided full colour bedroom door hanger.

Return this page **with six tokens per gift required** to:
Marketing Dept., MM / LM, World International Ltd.,
PO Box 7, Manchester, M19 2HD

Your name:_____ Age: _____

Address: _____

_____

_____ Postcode: _____

Parent / Guardian Name (Please Print)_____

Please tape a 20p coin to your request to cover part post and package cost

I enclose <u>six</u> tokens per gift, and 20p please send me:-

<u>Posters:-</u>　　Mr Men Poster ☐　　Little Miss Poster ☐

<u>Door Hangers</u> -　Mr Nosey / Muddle ☐　Mr Greedy / Lazy ☐

20p　　Mr Tickle / Grumpy ☐　Mr Slow / Busy ☐

Mr Messy / Quiet ☐　Mr Perfect / Forgetful ☐

L Miss Fun / Late ☐　L Miss Helpful / Tidy ☐

L Miss Busy / Brainy ☐　L Miss Star / Fun ☐

Stick 20p here please

We may occasionally wish to advise you of other Mr Men gifts.
If you would rather we didn't please tick this box ☐

Please Tick Appropriate Box

|--- 100 mm ---|

ENTRANCE FEE
3 SAUSAGES

250 mm

MR. GREEDY

Collect six of these tokens
You will find one inside every
Mr Men and Little Miss book
which has this special offer.

1
TOKEN

Offer open to residents of UK, Channel Isles and Ireland only

Mr Men and Little Miss Library Presentation Boxes

In response to the many thousands of requests for the above, we are delighted to advise that these are now available direct from ourselves, for only **£4.99** (inc VAT) plus 50p p&p.
The full colour boxes accommodate each complete library. They have an integral carrying handle as well as a neat stay closed fastener.
Please do not send cash in the post. Cheques should be made payable to **World International Ltd. for the sum of £5.49** (inc p&p) per box.

Please note books are not included.

Please return this page with your cheque, stating below which presentation box you would like, to:-
Mr Men Office, World International
PO Box 7, Manchester, M19 2HD

Your name:_____

Address: _____

_____

_____Postcode: _____

Name of Parent/Guardian (please print):_____

Signature:_____

I enclose a cheque for £_____ made payable to World International Ltd.,

Please send me a Mr Men Presentation Box ☐

               Little Miss Presentation Box ☐   (please tick or write in quantity) and allow 28 days for delivery

Thank you

Offer applies to UK, Eire & Channel Isles only

little Miss Naughty

by Roger Hargreaves

WORLD INTERNATIONAL

Are you ever naughty?

Sometimes, I bet!

Well, little Miss Naughty was naughty all the time.

She awoke one Sunday morning and looked out of the window.

"Looks like a nice day," she thought to herself.

And then she grinned.

"Looks like a nice day for being naughty," she said.

And rubbed her hands!

That Sunday Mr Uppity was out for his morning stroll.

Little Miss Naughty knocked his hat off his head.

And jumped on it!

"My hat!" cried Mr Uppity.

That afternoon Mr Clever was sitting in his garden reading a book.

And do you know what that little Miss Naughty did?

She broke his glasses!

"My glasses!" cried Mr Clever.

That evening Mr Bump was just standing there.

Minding his own business.

And guess what little Miss Naughty did?

She ran off with his bandages!

And bandaged up Mr Small!

"Mmmmmmmmmmmffffff!" he cried.

It's difficult to say anything when you're bandaged up like that!

Mr Uppity and Mr Clever and Mr Bump and Mr Small were very very very very cross.

Very very very very cross indeed!

"Oh what a wonderful Sunday," giggled little Miss Naughty as she walked along.

"And it isn't even bedtime yet!"

First thing on Monday morning the Mr Men had a meeting.

"Something has to be done," announced Mr Uppity, who had managed to straighten out his hat.

They all looked at Mr Clever, who was wearing his spare pair of glasses.

"You're the cleverest," they said. "What's to be done about little Miss Naughty?"

Mr Clever thought.

He cleared his throat.

And spoke.

"I've no idea," he said.

"I have," piped up Mr Small.

"I know what that naughty little lady needs," he went on.

"And I know who can do it," he added.

"What?" asked Mr Uppity.

"Who?" asked Mr Clever.

"Aha!" chuckled Mr Small, and went off to see a friend of his.

Somebody who could do impossible things.

Somebody who could do impossible things like making himself invisible.

I wonder who that could be?

That Monday Mr Nosey was asleep under a tree.

Little Miss Naughty crept towards him with a pot of paint in one hand, a paintbrush in the other, and a rather large grin on her face.

She was going to paint the end of his nose!

Red!

But.

Just as she was about to do the dreadful deed,
something happened.

TWEAK!

Somebody tweaked her nose!

Somebody she couldn't see tweaked her nose!

Somebody invisible!

I wonder who?

"Ouch!" cried little Miss Naughty.

And, dropping the paint and paintbrush,
she ran away as fast as her little legs would
carry her.

On Tuesday Mr Busy was rushing along.

As usual!

Little Miss Naughty, standing by the side of the road, stuck out her foot.

She was going to trip him up!

Head over heels!

And heels over head!

But.

Just before she did, something happened.

TWEAK!

The invisible nose tweaker had struck again!

And it hurt!

"Ouch!" cried little Miss Naughty.

And ran away even faster than her little legs would carry her.

On Wednesday Mr Happy was at home.

Watching television!

Outside, little Miss Naughty picked up a stone.

She was going to break his window!

Naughty girl!

But.

As she brought her arm back to throw, guess what?

That's right!

TWEAK!

"Ouch!" cried little Miss Naughty as she ran off holding her nose.

And so it went on.

All day Thursday.

TWEAK!

All day Friday.

TWEAK! TWEAK!

All day Saturday.

TWEAK! TWEAK! TWEAK!

By which time little Miss Naughty's nose was bright red.

But.

By Sunday she was cured.

No naughtiness at all!

Thanks to the invisible nose tweaker.

On Sunday evening Mr Small went round to see him.

"Hello Mr Impossible," he smiled.

"Thank you for helping to cure little Miss Naughty."

"My pleasure," laughed Mr Impossible.

"But it did take all week."

Mr Small grinned.

"Don't you mean," he said. "All tweak?"